This Peppa Pig book belongs to

....

This book is based on the
TV Series 'Peppa Pig'
'Peppa Pig' is created by
Neville Astley and Mark Baker

Peppa Pig © Astley Baker Davies/
Entertainment One UK Limited 2003

www.peppapig.com

Published by Ladybird Books Ltd 2011
A Penguin Company
Penguin Books Ltd, 80 Strand, London, WC2R 0RL, UK
Penguin Books Australia Ltd, Camberwell, Victoria, Australia
Penguin Books (NZ), 67 Appollo Drive, Rosedale, Auckland 0632,
New Zealand (a divison of Pearson New Zealand Ltd)

Contents

Use your colourful stickers to decorate the pages of this book or to add to your own pictures.

Help Peppa Pig to find 5 yellow ducks like this hidden in your book (The answers are on page 61).

Peppa's family

Can you make the sounds? Some are quite quiet, some are very loud.

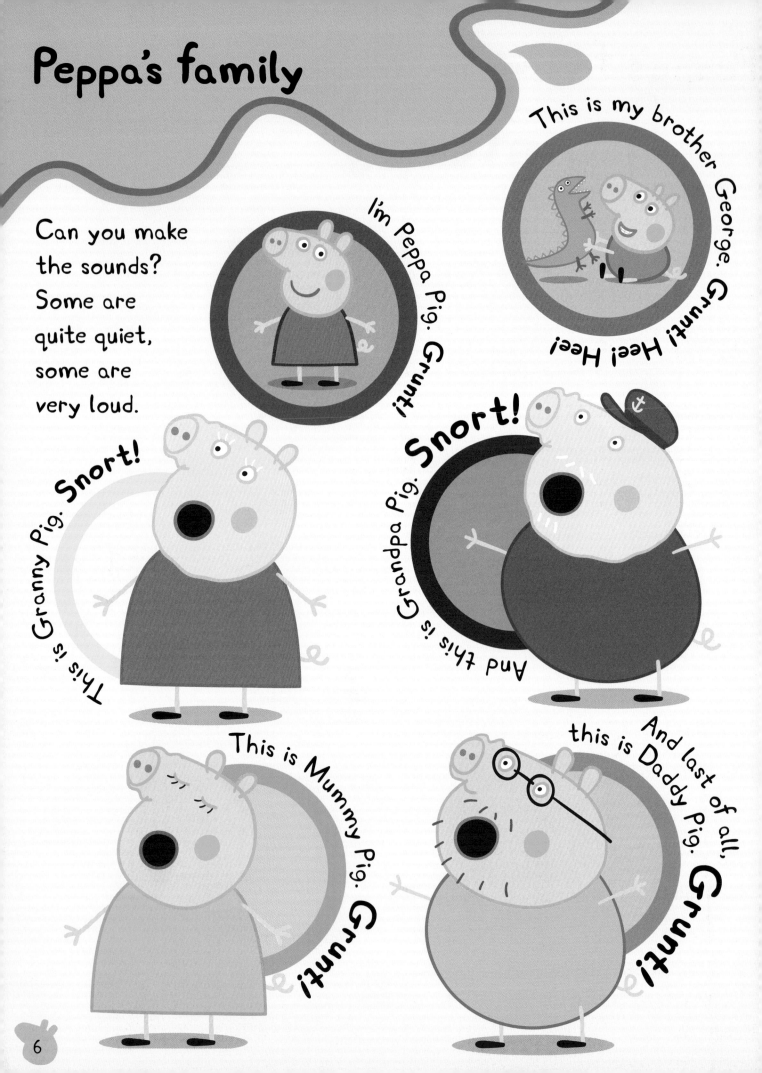

This is my brother George. Grunt! Hee! Hee!

I'm Peppa Pig. Grunt!

This is Granny Pig. **Snort!**

Snort! And this is Grandpa Pig.

This is Mummy Pig. Grunt!

And last of all, this is Daddy Pig. Grunt!

Peppa's friends

Draw lines to match up the picture of each friend with their name.

Emily Elephant

Zoe Zebra

Edmond Elephant

Suzy Sheep

Richard Rabbit

Danny Dog

Pedro Pony

Candy Cat

Doesn't Peppa have a lot of friends?
Peppa is your friend, too. What are your other friends called?

Writing names

Peppa loves writing her name. "Snort!"
Use a pencil to trace the five letters
in Peppa's name.

One letter appears three times in Peppa's
name. Do you know what letter this is?

Write your name here

Who's missing?

Peppa is watching her brother George and Daddy Pig riding on the big wheel. But someone is missing . . . It's you!

Draw a picture of yourself in the space below.

Granny Pig's chickens

Peppa Pig and George are very excited. Tonight they are sleeping at Granny and Grandpa Pig's house.

Peppa and George take a look at their bedroom. "It was your mummy's when she was a little piggy," Granny Pig explains.

Out in the garden Grandpa Pig proudly shows Peppa and George the vegetables he's grown. But there's a bare patch of earth where Grandpa's lettuces ought to be!

"Meet Jemima, Sarah and Vanessa," says Granny Pig, as three hens come to peck at the bare earth.

"Those hens ate my lettuces!" complains Grandpa Pig

Peppa and George give the chickens some corn and lead them back towards the chicken coop.

"Snort! Eat up!" cries Peppa.
Neville the cockerel comes over to see what is happening. "Cock-a-doodle-do!"
"Do!" says George.
"Let's see if you have a surprise for us in the morning," laughs Granny Pig.

At bedtime Peppa and George climb into Mummy Pig's old bed. It's very bouncy and comfy, and they sleep soundly until morning when . . .

. . . they are woken by Neville the cockerel's loud "Cock-a-doodle-dooooo!" Peppa and George race outside to the chicken coop.

11

They peep inside the coop.
"There are four eggs in the straw!"
grunts Peppa.
"Well done, Jemima, Sarah and
Vanessa," says Granny Pig. "That's
one egg each for breakfast."

"Snort! Thank you for waking
us up, Neville," says Peppa.
"Cock-a-doodle-do!"
"Do!" says George.
"And thank you, hens, for
our breakfast," Peppa says.
Peppa carefully
carries the eggs
inside, using her
granny's basket.

"Boiled eggs for everyone," calls Granny Pig when breakfast is ready. Peppa and George are hungry after all that running about and egg-collecting. Peppa eats a spoonful of her egg.
"Granny, your chickens make yummy eggs!"

Granny Pig explains that the corn Peppa and George fed the hens yesterday helps to make the eggs taste good.
"The eggs taste even better because Granny Pig's hens ate my lettuces!" grunts Grandpa Pig.
And everyone laughs – even Grandpa.

I-Spy colours

Help Peppa to spy the colours by pointing to all the reds, greens, pinks and yellows in this picture. Then finish colouring the picture.

Granny Pig's hens love to eat food that's coloured yellow.
Do you know what the food is called?

___ ___ ___ ___

Answer: corn

Picnic time!

What a lovely day for a picnic in the woods. Grunt!

Look at the small pictures around the edge of the big picture.
Can you spot all five inside the big picture?

Can you see one of Peppa's friends in the trees? What is she doing?

Tick each box when you find them.

Answer: Polly Parrot is twirling round a branch. Wheeee!

17

Delphine's visit

Peppa has a very good friend called Delphine Donkey, who lives in France. Look at the picture and word key below, then at the story on the opposite page. Every time you see one of the pictures in the story, say the word.

Key

Peppa

Delphine

suitcase

sleeping ZZZ z

car

friends

bed

train

George

travels by  to stay with .

Her  is very heavy! Daddy Pig puts the

on top of the  .

The  have a lovely time playing. But when

it's time for no one is Z Z Z z .

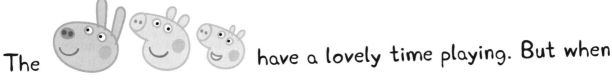 teaches and a French song called

Frère Jacques about Z Z Z z until morning.

It works! Yawn . . . Yawn . . . Snore! Snore!

Pairing puzzle

Peppa and her friends have lost their favourite toys. Can you help by tracing your finger along the lines to match the toys to their owners?

Spin the dice

You will need:
- Colouring pencils
- A dice

What does your favourite toy look like? Draw a picture here. Then find a dice and roll it to see what colours to use for the circles, squares and stars in the patterned border.

1 = red   2 = orange   3 = yellow

4 = blue   5 = purple   6 = green

Find the toys

Snort! Help Peppa and George find the beach ball, teddy, monkey and Mr Dinosaur before they go to the beach for the day.

Numbers

It's a school day for Peppa and her friends.
Madame Gazelle is their teacher. She is kind and helpful.
"Hello, children," says Madame Gazelle.
"Today we will be learning to count. Who wants to try?"
"Me! Me! Me!" all the children say.

Pedro Pony has the first try. "1, 2, 3, 4 . . ."
Then Rebecca Rabbit has a go. "1, 2, 3, 4, 5, 6, 7 . . ."
And, although it's quite hard, most of the children
manage to count all the way to ten,
"1, 2, 3, 4, 5, 6, 7, 8, 9, 10!"
Madame Gazelle is
very pleased. "Super!
It's playtime now,
so you can all
go outside."

Peppa and some of her friends want to play a skipping game.

Peppa sings this rhyme as she twirls the rope:
"I like sand,
I like sea,
I like Suzy to
skip with me!"

Then Suzy
Sheep sings:
"I like ping
And I like pong,
I like Zoe to
skip along!"

Rebecca Rabbit wants to see who can skip the longest.
"1, 2, 3, 4, 5, 6, 7, 8, 9, 10. Zoe wins!"

Peppa feels sad that she can't reach up to ten skips,
but then Emily Elephant comes along with her orange hula hoop.

Peppa and her friends count how many times Emily can swirl the hoop round her trunk - without stopping.

"Hee hee!" says Emily, as the hula hoop goes round and round and round.

"Wow! That's more than ten times," says Suzy. "I think that's about one hundred, actually."

"Snort! Snort!" Here comes George. He wants to play leapfrog. Peppa likes leapfrog, too. "Snort!"

The children line up, and George leaps over them one by one, just like a hoppity frog.

"1, 2, 3, 4, 5, 6, 7, 8, 9 . . . 10!"
they count.

At the end of playtime they tell Madame Gazelle that they can all count to ten now, and that they learn best when they are playing. "Super," says Madame Gazelle. "Let's play a counting game with the big skipping rope."

Just then, Daddy Pig arrives to collect Peppa and George. He joins in with the skipping and counting game.
"Snort! Grunt! Hee! hee!" say Peppa and George. They love school and counting, especially when their daddy plays skipping with them!

Number bricks

Peppa and her friends are playing with numbered bricks. Emily has made a pretend rocket with them. Look at the picture and answer the questions below.

How many bricks have number 5 on them?

How many friends are there (including Peppa)?

How many bricks are there on the floor?

What colour is the number 3 brick?

Answers: Three bricks have number 5 on them; there are eight friends altogether; there are four bricks on the floor; the number 3 brick is green.

Yummy puzzle

Peppa and George like ice cream, especially on a hot day. Today Peppa chose vanilla and George chose chocolate. **Snort! Snort!**

Which flavour will their friends choose? Find out by tracing your finger along the lines.

strawberry   blueberry   tutti-frutti

Ice cream dream

What is your favourite ice cream flavour? Dream up the best ice cream in the world and draw a picture of it here.

Tear out photos of cool treats from old magazines to make a zingy picture frame.

Snow-time!

Peppa and her friends love playing in the snow. And so does Daddy Pig! Look at this scene and answer the questions.

Snort!

Grunt!

What colour hat, scarf, gloves and boots would you like to wear to play in the snow?

How many hats can you see?

Yippeeeeeeee!

Count all the boots. How many are there?

Who is wearing green boots, gloves, hat and scarf?

What colour scarf is Danny Dog wearing?

How many friends are riding on sledges?

Answers: There are six hats. There are twelve boots; Daddy Pig is wearing green boots, gloves, hat and scarf; three friends are riding on sledges; Danny Dog's scarf is turquoise.

Bouncy castle puzzler

At the school fête Peppa Pig, George and friends have their faces painted
They all decide to be tigers, and it's hard to tell them apart.

Hee-hee!

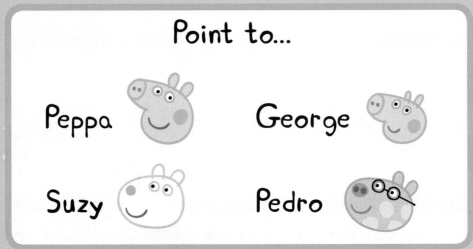

Point to...

Peppa

George

Suzy

Pedro

There are five differences between these two pictures.
Can you spot them all?

Grandpa's compost

Today Daddy Pig is chopping vegetables
to make soup. Peppa wants to help.
"Thank you, Peppa," says Daddy Pig.
"Please throw away the vegetable leftovers for me."
"Grunt! Hee! Hee!" says Peppa, as she begins scraping
the peelings into the normal rubbish bin.

"Stop, Peppa!" says Mummy Pig.
"Put them in the green bin, please."
"Na-na-na," says George, taking
a banana skin from the compost bin.
"That's right, George," says
Mummy Pig.

"The banana skin can be recycled,
which means used for something else."
"What else?" Peppa asks.

"Let's ask Grandpa Pig," says Mummy Pig, as they drive to Granny and Grandpa's house.

"Do you like eating banana skins?" Peppa asks her Grandpa.

"No, but my plants will grow tall and healthy if I put the leftover fruit and vegetables into my compost box . . . with a little help from my friends the worms, of course."

Peppa and George dig a big hole.

"Wiggle, wiggle!" giggles George as he finds another worm to put in the compost box.

"Snort! I've found one too!" says Peppa, and she sings this song:

" You're a wriggly worm
You're a wriggly worm
How do you do, I love you
You're a wriggly worm! "

37

Peppa and George drop their worms on top of the leftovers from Daddy Pig's soup.
"Be a good wriggly worm and turn it all into compost!" Peppa whispers to her worm.
"Wiggle, wiggle!" says George, as Granny Pig calls them to the orchard where she's busy picking fruit.

"Just look at those rosy apples!" says Granny Pig. "They've had lots of compost to help them grow." When Peppa and George try to pick apples too, they can't reach the branches.
Mummy Pig smiles. "I think Granny and Grandpa have a little trick to help you."

"One, two, three . . .
Shake the tree!"

And down come lots of apples for Peppa and George to collect . . . and to eat!

"Grunt! Yum! Yum!"

"Now I know where to throw the apple cores," says Peppa.

"Wiggle, wiggle," says George, and they race back to Grandpa Pig's compost box.

Peppa and George throw their apple cores on top of the vegetable peelings.

"Please make more yummy food for the plants and trees," Peppa whispers to her worm.

"Hee! Hee!" What a lovely time they've had in Granny and Grandpa's garden.

Autumn fun!

Peppa and her family love to roll around in the crisp autumn leaves. **Hee! Hee!**

Colour the woolly coats, hats and scarves using the key:

r = red   y = yellow   o = orange

9 = green   p = pink   b = blue

These words appeared in the story about Grandpa's compost box. Do you remember them? Join the dots to write the words.

box   wiggle

worm

Can you spot four worms and a snail hiding under the leaves?

Play pretend

Peppa and George have a dressing-up box.

They are playing pretend. Peppa lives in a castle.

Snort! Imagine that - it's brave Princess Peppa and brave Knight George!

After a very scary adventure (where they saved Suzy Sheep), Princess Peppa and Knight George return to the castle.

All their friends cheer. Hooray!

Why don't you dress up in your favourite costume and pretend to be anything, or anyone, you want?

Balloon maze

Start

Peppa and her family are taking an exciting ride in a hot-air balloon. Help them find their way across the sky and safely down to the ground. Use your finger to weave between all the clouds.

Where would you fly in a balloon?

Finish

Space adventure

Daddy Pig, Peppa, Mummy Pig, George and Edmond Elephant are on a space ride.

Oink! Oink! Oink! Whooosh!

Draw a picture of yourself in the pilot's seat and write your name along the dotted line. Colour in the planets and stars!

Shoe shopping

Peppa is shopping for shoes with Mummy Pig.
She likes the red pumps best, but the left one is missing.
Help Peppa by searching along the shelves to find it.

Bubble bath

Peppa loves her new shoes so much that she keeps them on in the bath!

How many bubbles can you count in the picture?

Answer: There are twenty-six bubbles.

Slippy ice

Some of the words are missing from this poem about Peppa's day at the ice rink. Every time you see a missing word, find it in the box below then say it out loud as part of the whole poem.

very hurt

Peppa

George

ice sweet

well Hooray

Grunt! Grunt!

Colour Peppa and her friends' lovely woolly hats.

Peppa tried the _ _ _

But it wasn't _ _ _ _ _ nice.

It _ _ _ _ _ when she fell.

But didn't she do _ _ _ _ _ ?

Mummy Pig helped _ _ _ _ _ _

get back on her feet.

Peppa helped _ _ _ _ _ _ _ get up, too.

Isn't that _ _ _ _ _ _ !

Soon they were both skating. Grunt! Grunt! _ _ _ _ _ _ _

All in all, it turned out to be a very nice day!

Woody I-Spy

Peppa and her family are spotting creatures in the woods. Look at the four small pictures around the edge of the big picture. Can you spot the small pictures inside the big picture? Tick the boxes when you find them.

"Oink! Dino-saw!"

Oh, no! George has lost Mr Dinosaur. Can you help find him?

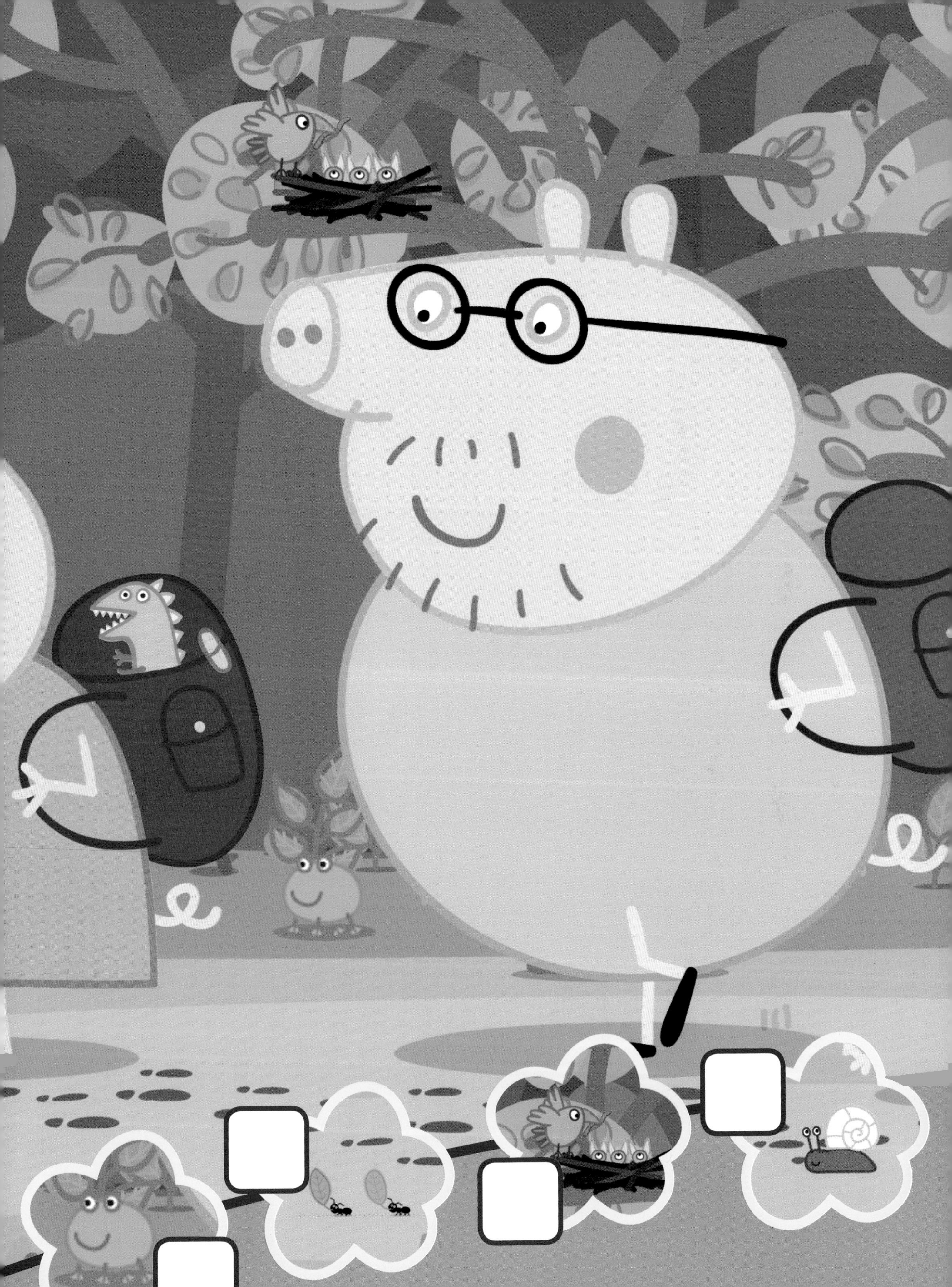

Answer: George's dinosaur is in Mummy Pig's rucksack.

School camp

Peppa Pig and her school friends are camping. Madame Gazelle, their teacher, is looking after them.

Madame _azelle

_edro Pony

_anny Dog

Write in the missing letters of the names, to show who is sleeping in each tent.

G P C
D S R P

_eppa Pig

_uzy Sheep

_ichard Rabbit

_andy Cat

Danny's pirate party

Today is Danny Dog's birthday. He's having a pirate party.
"Yo, ho, ho!" cries Danny as his friends arrive. They are dressed as swashbuckling pirates.
"Grunt! Yo, ho, ho!" says Peppa Pig.

"Yee-ha!" says Pedro, who is dressed as a cowboy.
"Grunt! Yee-ha!" shouts Peppa.
The room turns silent when a BIG shape appears in the doorway.
A gruff pirate voice announces, "Ahoy there! Me name's Dog Beard!"

"I thought your name was Grandad Dog," says Peppa. "Sshh," says Grandad Dog. "Today me name's Dog Beard, and I be on the lookout for brave pirates to come adventuring with me." The children look puzzled.

Danny's grandad explains. "That nasty Captain Hog, he stole me treasure. Will you help me get it back from the orchard where it's hidden?"

"Arrrr!" cry Danny Dog and Peppa.

But Suzy Sheep says, "Captain Hog sounds scary."

Peppa smiles. "Grandpa Pig has an orchard with fruit trees. I bet Grandpa is pretending to be Captain Hog."

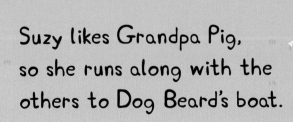

Suzy likes Grandpa Pig, so she runs along with the others to Dog Beard's boat.

"Yo, ho, ho!" cheer the children as they put on their life jackets and climb on board. "Anchors away!" calls Dog Beard as they sail in the direction of the treasure.

"Land ahoy!" cries Dog Beard when they spy an orchard ahead. The pirate friends creep off the boat and look for the treasure. They must find it without being caught by that nasty Captain Hog.

Everyone manages to find
some treasure. It's coins
made from chocolate!
"Yum!" says Peppa
as she tries one.
"Baa!"
"Woof!"
"Oink!"
The treasure is delicious
and soon everyone has
chocolatey mouths.

When Mummy Dog carries in a chocolate birthday cake for Danny Dog,
the pirates sing a Happy Birthday song. The grown-up pirates, Dog Beard
and Captain Hog, sing along too.
"More chocolate!" says Danny. "This be the best pirate party ever! Woof!"
"Arrrr!" says Peppa.
And everyone agrees. "Arrrrrrrrrr!"

59

Rainbow!

It's a wet day today. Mummy Pig and Daddy Pig have their umbrellas to keep them dry. But Peppa and George like getting wet. Colour the rainbow and add patterns and colours to the umbrellas, then draw lots more raindrops to make the day even wetter.

Did you find five yellow ducks in your book?

The yellow ducks are hidden on pages:
23, 28, 41, 49 and 58.